Singing with Elephants

Singing with Elephants

Elephants

MARGARITA ENGLE

VIKING

VIKING
An imprint of Penguin Random House LLC, New York

First published in the United States of America by Viking, an imprint of
Penguin Random House LLC, 2022

Visit us online at penguinrandomhouse.com.

Library of Congress Cataloging-in-Publication Data is available.

Printed in the United States of America

ISBN 9780593206690

1st Printing

LSCH

Edited by Liza Kaplan
Design by Monique Sterling
Text set in Goudy Old Style

For teachers
and future teachers
with gratitude, admiration, and hope

POETRY IS A DANCE

of words on the page.

These poems are a story
about the summer
I learned
how to twirl
and leap
on paper.

It was the summer when I met a famous poet
and a family of musical elephants.

Until then, all I could do was wish
like a caged songbird
 wordless
 wistful
 wishful . . .

SANTA BARBARA, CALIFORNIA

~ 1947 ~

MUSICAL ELEPHANTS ARE LIKE

mountains with windy whispers,
the sea when it roars or chants a lullaby,
tree branches that clack like maracas,
and every animal that opens its mouth
to howl, bark, or chant
about the freedom
to walk, walk, walk,
rejoicing in the sheer joy
of touching
green earth
with rhythmic feet
and dancing
minds.

ONE DAY

I'm rhythmically walking, walking, walking,
with various creatures on comically tangled
leashes, when we reach the garden of a cozy-looking
house
right across from the high school, and there, kneeling
as if in prayer
is a stranger.

She's old, but her face looks strong.
I wonder if my own dark eyebrows
are as winged as hers
ready to rise
and fly
like feathers.

Pleased to meet you, I say in English.

She glances up.

This is my giant wolfhound Flora
and my miniature goat Fauna, but the piglets
and ducklings are just temporary patients
from our veterinary clinic
where my parents are the doctors
and I'm almost a sort of eleven-year-old nurse
because I feed, clean, pet, cuddle, walk, walk, walk,

and sometimes I even help with unusual animals
at a wildlife zoo-ranch
where adventurous movies
are often filmed.
I'm going to be a healer one day . . .

My voice
trails away
when I see her frown
   and glance down at her notebook
and realize—
I have disturbed her.

I DON'T BELONG HERE

The stranger studies me.

What is she thinking?
Is she wise?
Could we be friends?

I wonder
whether
I've said
too much,
made
too many
mistakes
in inglés.

I wonder . . .

Would this woman care
if I told her
about the girls at school
who make fun
of me for being
   small
   brownish
   chubby

with curly black hair barely tamed
by a long braid?

Would she care that the girls at school
call me
    zoo beast
when my clean clothes
smell a bit like animals?

Would she care that the boys call me
    ugly
    stupid
    tongue-tied
because my accent gets stronger
when I'm nervous, like when
the teacher forces me to read
out loud?

I wonder.

IF ONLY THE WRITER

could speak my true language.

She does!
Te gusta la poesía, she says,
telling me that I like poetry
Her español is rhythmic like a song,
slower than mine, and fancier,
with words that sound like they
belong in a book, which is what
she says she's writing—
a volume of verses.

Voy a adivinar, she says—I'm going to guess.
Vienes para aprender a escribir la poesía.
You've come to learn how to write poetry.

Should I answer honestly?
I simply shrug, embarrassed to admit
that I came for many reasons,
to see who
she is
and what
she's doing,
and because I'm
lonely.

PERHAPS SHE CAN SEE

inside my heart.
Because she doesn't tell me to leave,
just says
I will teach you
like I haven't bothered her at all,
like it's no big deal I'm here.

I tell her my classmates say
I ask too many questions.

Ay, no, she insists—no importa,
she will teach me a bit about writing.

Poetry is like a planet, she says,
each word spins
    orbits
    twirls
    and radiates
reflected
starlight.

If you want to write, you have to observe
movements, and absorb
stillness.

She smiles, and reaches to pat Flora's
huge head, which only encourages my sloppy dog
to lick her hand, while Fauna just does what goats
always do, nibbles on the edges of the notebook,
and the hem of la poeta's dress, and a button
on her blouse.

I pull all the animals away
before they can start eating her hair.

ME ENCANTAN TODAS LAS BESTIECITAS

I love all animals,
the poetry teacher says.

I smile, because animals
are my family's whole life,
now that my grandma
is gone.

I wonder if the poetry teacher
would like to see my parents' clinic
after my poetry lesson.

Do you write in English or in Spanish?
I ask.
I tell her I've been trying to
practice English for school,
but Spanish feels like home.

Una mezcla, la poeta suggests,
let us mix our languages together
like emotions that swirl and blend
in a pot of paint, azul y rojo
becoming purple, amarillo y azul
turning to green.

LANGUAGE IS A MYSTERY

After a whole year in California,
español is still the only way of speaking
that feels completely natural to me,
letters like ñ and *rr*
hidden inside my island-mind
where words are so much more alive
than in my incomplete
immigration-mouth.

The poet switches to inglés
just to help me—but animals
don't recognize my effort
to make sense
of letters like a *y*
that sounds like my *ll*
and an *h* that is not silent
and a *k* that does not even exist
in Spanish—so todas las bestiecitas
begin to bark, bleat, quack, and grunt
   a humorous animal opera
so ridiculous and endearing that for the first time
since Abuelita's funeral, I actually chuckle
and laugh out loud—a genuine
carcajada, a guffaw!

How wondrous it feels
to remember that laughter
has no language, and can cross
any boundary line,
even the wavy ones
between species.

CHILD OF THE ARK

Each time I leave our clinic-house
with assorted creatures on leashes,
my big sister, Catalina, says I look
like a refugee from Noah's Ark.

I call her Cat, and she calls me Olivia—
    a mythical saint who never
    actually existed; but Abuelita loved to imagine
    that she was a real woman who carried
    an olive branch for peace—
but to everyone else, I'm Oriol.

My bird name
musical and sweet,
is one I chose
for myself, long ago in Cuba,
when
I knew who I was
and how
to speak.

MY WISHING WINDOW

Now, here in this foreign country
with Abuelita above me in Heaven,
all I have left that belonged to her
is a little blue glass statuette
    a figurine
    an elephant
that sparkles
like starlight.

When she gave me el elefante,
she told me to put it on my windowsill
where its curved trunk could reach up
and catch good luck.

Each morning and evening,
I whisper my wish to move back
to Cuba,
and I wait . . .

WE MOVED TO CALIFORNIA

because Abuelita
needed a specialized diabetes
research medical center,
but los médicos failed to save her
so I don't understand why we should stay.

Will we ever move back to Cuba?

No, Mima says. Ay, no, mijita, Papi sighs.
Never, my sister assures me, no way,
our parents are happy here
with the wide variety of animals
                    wild ones
                    and pets
that depend on them for medicine
and stitches and braces
and encouragement
and all the other marvels
veterinarians depend on
to heal, mend, and befriend.

THE ONLY GOOD LUCK

in my life right now
comes in the form of
accidental poetry lessons
from a wise old poeta
because I never told her
why I was really there . . .

But Abuelita always said the best stories
begin with había y no había—
    there was
    and there was not—
like fairy tales
that mix history
with magic.
Maybe that's how
my scribbled efforts
will end up,
    both real
    and daydreamed
like a blue glass statuette
dancing on paper.

Some poems stay in the mind.
Others end up on paper.

CONFESSION

The next day when I kneel
beside the scribbler, happy animals
play all around us.

She sets her notebook aside
and gives me her full attention,
as if she thinks that one stray,
roaming child
is worth
as much
as a verse.

Why do you prefer Oriol? she asks,
adding, Someday maybe I'll tell you
how and why I chose my own name.

My answer is simple:
birds are sweeter
than people.

That's when I tell her about school,
and insults, and my accent, and how much
I dread September, when I will have to read
OUT LOUD again.

La poeta replies quietly, saying that bullies
are bullies because they were bullied.

Hate fades, she explains, but love
lasts forever.

I'm not sure exactly what she means,
but I do know that animals show me
when they're grateful, even if
only a few minutes earlier,
they thought I was
their enemy.

GRATITUDE

The veterinary clinic fills up most of our house,
with rooms full of crates, kennels, and surgical tables,
our entire garden a pasture where donkeys and calves
graze in tidy corrals.

Just last week, I was embraced by an injured swan
after my parents saved its life.

I've been hugged by many four-footed creatures,
but that was my first experience being enclosed
within the soft strength of wings.

There is no better subject for your first poem,
says la poeta during one of our lessons,
than prayers answered and wishes fulfilled.
El cisne was grateful for food and shelter as well as
la medicina, just as you are so thankful
for all the sights, sounds, touches, tastes,
and smells of nature.
¿Verdad?

Yes, that's true!
How did she know that I love everything
about the outdoors?

CHOICES

Crowded in my room with animals all around me,
I wonder about wishes
and prayers.
Is there a difference between the two?

That evening
I make a new wish:
to compose words
that dance on paper,
like the ones my poet-friend
writes, and then recites.

Then I pray for courage
    at school in the fall,
    for bravery now,
    each time one of the
    four-legged patients at our clinic
    fails to survive.

Maybe a wish
and a prayer
are just different words
    different ways
of asking for something better.

THE DAILY DICTIONARY

When your parents are veterinarians
you learn new words every day,
vocabulary that comes from Latin
    canine for dogs
    equine for horses
    avian for birds
    feline for cats.

Pachyderm is the term
for elephants,
but it's Greek, not Latin,
and it includes rhinos and tapirs
even though they're not related,
just big.

Lots of scientific words were invented
a long time ago.
I try to remember
that when I help Papi
float the teeth of a racehorse
    an old-fashioned
way of saying that we're filing teeth,
because *float* is a word left over
from the olden days
when bricklayers
made the tops of garden walls level

by filing
rough bricks.

I wonder if the words
for different kinds of verses
of poetry
will make just as much
old-fashioned sense
as zoological
curiosities.

TODAY, LA POETA

taught me about onomatopoeia,
which she said is just a way of saying *growl*
by writing *grrrrr*, and *howl* by substituting
aaaaaoooooooo.

She said it's fine if I only want to make vowels
rhyme, instead of whole words, and las rimas
can come in the middles of lines, instead of
at the ends.

Poetry,
she said,
can be whatever you want it
to be.

POETRY FROM ANIMALS

So I listen
listen
listen
and watch
watch
watch
as my dog
and my goat
use paws
and hooves
to pound out
a drum song
while we
walk
walk
walk.

We're on our way to study la poesía
with the neighbor who knows both
inglés and Spanish, but I feel like
I'm traveling toward friendship
instead.

MEMORIES FOLLOW ME

If only my entire mind
felt light and clear
like the scribbler's
musical verses.

Last year before we moved here,
Cuba was home, Abuelita was alive,
español was my only language,
and I was never very lonely
because cousins flowed
in and out of our house
like ruffled flocks
of prancing
flamingos.

I don't know what to do with these
stormy downpours of loneliness.

Put them into a verse, la poeta advises.
There is no better home for emotions
than a poem, which can easily be transformed
into a song.

She speaks as if she knows.
And I wonder
if she does.

AT LEAST IT'S SUMMER NOW

The worst thing about my new school
was not being called zoo beast or ugly
or stupid.

It was being placed in a baby class—
third grade instead of fifth—by a foolish
teacher, who assumed that I could not
ever
learn inglés
simply because
I had not learned it
yet.

Ever and *yet* are two words
that la poeta says I must remember,
in order to keep myself from imagining
that the first is permanent
or the second
impossible.

EACH TIME I VISIT THE POET

I learn something new.
A word.
Or a rhythm.
A rhyme.
Or a melody.

La poeta is so full of música
that over and over, she shows me
how to make a verse sound
alegre/happy
with verbs
like *soar*
or triste/sad
with nouns
like *ash* . . .

or more often
than I would have guessed
both triste/alegre combined
at the same time
just like my memories
of Abuelita
and la isla.

GIFTS

Abuelita always said I had a good ear
for bird communication—I could identify
any pajarito by its song, without looking up
or even opening
my eyes.

She said it was the gift of listening,
which is not the same as the gift
of a beautiful voice.

So instead of singing along when la poeta
reads her verses out loud,
I just listen
    imagine myself
dancing to the music of her song.

And I realize
that birds speak poetry
too—
without any words
at all.

HALF A GIFT

Not every animal makes
music.
I usually know what Flora wants
when she whines, or what Fauna
is begging for with an imploring
bleat, and I understand some
of the various hoots and cackles
made by owls and wild turkeys
that end up in our clinic
after the poor creatures
have been shot
or hit by a car
or attacked
by a puma.

I guess you could say I have a gift
for listening, but what about all the ways
animals communicate by wriggling, wagging,
jumping, and running?
How will I learn
to understand all those gestures and gazes?

When I ask la poeta, she advises me
to keep asking huge questions,
and don't stop until I receive an answer.

CRUELTY

The wildlife ranch where my parents
spend more and more of their time
    when they're not working at the clinic
is big and bold, but the enclosures
are tiny.

Mima and Papi keep writing to the owners—
who are Hollywood film stars—warning them
that lions and wolves need room to run,
not just pace, pace, pace back and forth
until they are sorrowful.

Chimpanzees and orangutans
look especially tragic in cramped cages
where they're forced to wear clothes,
eat with spoons, and pretend to grin
at laughing visitors from movie studios.

If you look closely,
you can see
those grins are actually
grimaces.

KINDNESS

Sometimes
Mima lets me come to the ranch with her.
Both there and at the clinic, she shows me how
she treats a monkey's toothache.

Papi lets me watch as he heals
the infected hoof of a reindeer.

Cat invites me
to help her pour ice into the warm pool
where an overheated polar bear droops
instead of swimming.

One morning I feed carrots to a mama giraffe,
admiring
her
long
blue
tongue.

The next day I toss flakes of hay
over the fence, into a small corral
where a lone zebra dreams of galloping
with his herd, on a natural savanna.

It feels so good to be helpful
        useful
        kind.

SOME DAYS FEEL STORMY

Clear sky, warm sun, but all the animals
are rebellious—Flora chases a skunk,
Fauna runs away with a llama,
a peacock flies all over the clinic
spraying enormous poops on the walls,
and even worse, some stupid human
throws an adorable puppy over our fence,
treating it like trash
instead of an orphan.

We'll find her a home, of course,
after I give Flora a tomato-juice bath,
and train her as a search dog to sniff the trail
left by Fauna and the llama, and wash,
wash, wash
stains
from walls.

No time for poetry lessons today.
Maybe tomorrow, life will rhyme.

WINDOW WISHES

Each morning I make a wish
to sing on paper
like the poet, then I watch sunlight
turn into rainbows as it enters
the prism of my little glass
elefante
in la ventana.

I think of Abuelita,
and the way we walked
and whistled along with all
the caged and free birds of Cuba.

Then I feed Flora and Fauna,
play with animals in the corrals
and kennels of the clinic, and finally
I walk, walk, walk, with tangled leashes
to take dogs, goats, the llama
to visit the scribbler
beneath her trees
where I can practice
making music of words.

SKILLS I HAVE NOT PERFECTED YET

Pronouncing English.
Fighting off sadness
whenever memories
chase me.

Struggling for precise words
to describe how the poet's verses
make me feel.

Struggling to write verses
of my own that capture
my heart.

What do I long for, she asks,
and all I can think of is:
    1. to belong
    2. to be brave

Even if wishes
sometimes come true,
I know we'll never
move back to Cuba.

¡A BAILAR!/TO DANCE!

Words, the scribbler tells me,
are a musical world.

They don't have to rhyme,
but sometimes they almost do,
and then there's a rhythm
that may or may not come
from counting syllables
and lines.

So I think of ballet
y la rumba, y el mambo—
all are dances, but each
offers its own
special manera
de bailar.

If I keep practicing the art of scribbling
rhythmically, beneath shady trees, then maybe
someday I'll be
una poeta
like my teacher.

CONVERSATION WITH AN OLD POET

ME: What are you writing about?
   Why do you write outdoors?
   Why do you kneel,
      don't you like chairs?

HER: I'm writing a long verse of nostalgia for my native
land
of mountains, villages, and children, a valley
called Elqui in the distant country of Chile,
where the people are like me—mestizos,
a mixture of Incas from the Andes mountains
and Basques from northern Spain.
I have never written a poem indoors
because I need a view of trees,
and I kneel
to touch madre tierra, Mother Earth.
Chairs are fine for reading in a room,
but poets also love
the comforting
discomforts
of nature.
This poem will dance on paper
long after I become an invisible spirit
twirling through air.

CONVERSATION WITH MYSELF

Old poets are as strange as bestiecitas,
speaking in a way that makes sense
on their own tongue,
even when it's difficult for others to
understand.

So I ask myself questions
before I ask her:

Is it possible to combine las ciencias
with la poesía so that I can become
a seriously scientific animal doctor
and a dance-on-paper
twirling poeta
at the same time?

SOME PEOPLE HAVE FAMILIES
MADE OF COMPANIONS

Today when I show up
for my daily lesson,
the poet is not alone.

Who is this woman
who acts
like a sister
or a husband,
some sort of relative
devoted and protective?

This is Doris,
mi secretaria, mi amiga,
she says.

Together, la poeta and her friend,
her secretaria
seem contented to divide their labor.
Doris doing everything indoors
like cooking and letter-writing,
while her boss kneels
beneath trees
scribbling verses
that sound like a whistling

birdsong breeze as it dances
with the leaves.

I try to enjoy
the peace
and stillness
    outdoors
but there are
too many thoughts
    inside my head.

WAVES OF WISHES

I leave la poeta
keep going downhill, all the way to the beach
where sunlight makes the water shimmer
as brightly as a blue glass elephant's lucky trunk
rising
and falling
over and over
with a rhythm
like music,
a poem
without
words.

I want to ask
    Abuelita to come back from the clouds
    the old poet to teach me about tree songs
    someone
    anyone
        how to be myself
        in a place
        where I don't
        belong.

And how to figure out
who I'm supposed to be.

CONVERSATION WITH MY PARENTS

ME: Can a scientist be poetic
without ignoring facts?

MIMA: ¡Ay, pero sí! When I was your age,
I read poemas by old-time naturalists
who were not required to specialize.

PAPI: ¿Poesía, por qué? Why?
Are you feeling emotional?

ME: I want to describe how it feels
to kneel on brown earth
with a view of green treetops
and blue sky . . .

PAPI: Entonces sí, once your chores are already done,
and only if you don't have too much homework,
yes, of course, go ahead and write.

ME: It's summer, no homework, just time and space
to explore.

CONVERSATION WITH MY
TEENAGE SISTER

ME: I met a strange lady who writes poems
so enthusiastically that you would think
she needed the words to keep herself alive.

CAT: Maybe she does. Maybe she thinks *you're* strange.
By the way, my new friend is coming over soon.
    Don't embarrass me.

I ignore the insult.
ME: She scribbles in the shade of trees.
I think in the fall I should do my homework
outdoors.

CAT: Shhh. There he is!

ME: *He??*

CAT: Yes. Surey. He's gentle and handsome, with black eyes
and black hair, and skin the same color as ours,
sixteen, the same as me, but he's been working
since he was your age.

ME: Wait, do Mima and Papi know you have a novio?
What's his name, can I meet him, does he like
animals, when will you marry him?

CAT: Your questions are always too nosy!
And don't you dare tell Mami and Papi
about my boyfriend, and don't call her Mima.

    It's just a weird word that means she
spoils us, but I'm not a baby.
But you, well,
you're you
just a silly child,
so young that you
can't understand
anything
important.

Anyway, he's a mahout
who trains elephants
at the ranch.
He came here from Nepal,
which is a little kingdom between India and China,
and the elephant he trains is called Chandra.
She's pregnant.
You'll meet her.
Soon.
But only if you promise
not to embarrass me
with ridiculous questions
and before you even ask—Surey means *sun*
and Chandra means *moon* in Nepali.

WONDERING

Cat is tall, slender, and so pretty
it's hard to believe we're related,
but her way of sharing information quickly
is just like mine, whenever I need
to reveal
my thoughts,
worries
or wonders . . .

A pregnant elephant!
A newborn pachyderm!
Will I be allowed to touch, feed, brush,
maybe even train
the baby?

REASSURANCE

Cat says her boyfriend
never uses a metal hook
or thick
leather whip
like elephant tamers
in zoos and the circus.

I learn that Surey grew up
in a forest with Chandra,
and when the elephant
was captured
by greedy exporters
he came here with her
so that she would not be frightened
or lonely—

Chandra was trained with love
and patience, not the brute force
humans use to bully
smaller countries
and other
species.

IMPATIENCE

Cat is older and maybe a little bit wise,
so I treasure everything she says
about her boyfriend
and his elephant.

I'm so eager to meet them
that I stay awake at night
wishing, wishing, wishing
   to belong
   to be brave
and then I add a wish
to find my place alongside
   teenagers
   grown-ups
   animals
   poets . . .

BETWEEN SKY AND EARTH

The morning brings
another lesson, another mystery.
The next word I learn from la poeta
is *el condor*, the name of an immense vulture
that soars above us
on an invisible
column of air
that swirls
like
a
whirlwind.

In Chile we have Andean condors, la poeta says,
and here there are these California condors,
slightly smaller but still enormous,
like flames
or sunbeams
that glow in midair
between worlds,
belonging nowhere
and everywhere.

METAPHORS

I gaze up at the huge dark bird.
How can she say it glows
when its ominous shape looks
like a symbol of death?

Metaphors, the poet explains,
describe the feeling when you see
something that is not
the thing itself.

Metaphors
are shadows
of words.

They are—
and they are not—
tangible
touchable
solid.

Like a grown-up elephant
is a mountain of strength?
I ask.

Yes! Exactamente,
the poet says.

And I am an echo
of the place where I used to live?

Ay, sí, yes, we are all echoes
of our younger selves.

SIMILES ARE DIFFERENT

Poets often use words that are like stories,
she adds, fairy tales you imagine
right before
they come true.

Similes are like doors
you can open to see worlds
that seem to be both ancient
and new.

Similes are like animals
that want to speak to you
and be understood
in their own language
instead of yours.
For instance, a bird's morning song
is like a festival of wordless sound
to welcome
the sun.

ASTONISHING WORDS

In just one day, I've learned
that condors fly between worlds

and metaphors are islands of answers
in an ocean of questions

and similes
are like songs
hummed by
elephants
made
of
glass
filled
with light.

I'm starting to think that maybe poems
exist in a world all their own, flowing
back and forth between reality
and wishes.

THE SHADE BENEATH TREES

summer heat
whispery leaves

air that dances
and sings
on paper

I feel
like a shadow
made of daydreams

MY ISLAND OF WHISTLING
BIRD-WALKERS

When I think about
our old life in my true home on la isla de Cuba
it now sounds metaphorical,
a once-upon-a-time
fairy tale's shadow,
but of course everything
was completely real,
or so I imagine.

Abuelita and I often communicated in Silba,
a whistled language her ancestors brought
from the Canary Islands near the coast of Africa.

We carried bamboo cages to the park
where our birds competed against others

until a winner was chosen by crowds
of cheering men.

I was always the only bird girl
in those male competitions.

Abuelita
said it was
because I am

brave enough
to lose.

So I've walked around
with that quiet feeling
of trying and failing
ever since then,
always hoping
that there will be
one more chance
to really believe
in something—
and win.

WHEN WISHES GROW

maybe
all I need
is a purpose

it's a word
filled with echoes
of other words
like courage
and hope

EVERYTHING BEGINS TO MAKE SENSE

On the evening of that same glorious day
when la poeta and I watch
a sky-dancing condor,
I return home
and discover
that my whole family
is gathered around
the kitchen table,
discussing a newspaper article
so surprising that I gasp as
Mima reads out loud,
about a famous writer who lives in a house
across from the high school, and is not only
the world's most famous poet, but also
a diplomat, who tries to help keep peace
between countries by making sure
the big ones don't bully
smaller nations.

According to the newspaper, the poet
chose to put down roots in Santa Barbara over
Los Angeles, because she prefers small towns
with lots of trees
and friendly neighbors.

A quiet life, she told the reporter,
is so much better
for poetry.

The article says she also came here
for the diabetes research facility
where she hopes to find
a cure.

This last part makes my heart plunge
down to my feet—

la poeta
has the same disease that killed Abuelita.

LA POETA FAMOSA

Once I've learned that my
accidental poesía teacher
is la famosa Gabriela Mistral,
the first Latin American winner
of the Nobel Prize for Literature—
and also one of the first women
to receive that award—
I race to the library to learn
more about her.
I learn that her mamá named her
Lucila de María Godoy Alcayaga,
but her nombre de pluma
that she chose herself
is a feathery pen name
for signing books:
Gabriela like the angel Gabriel—
and Mistral, a wild wind
that carries readers
far away.

EXCITEMENT

First a pregnant elephant,
and now this new joy I've
gained by learning that I've been
studying la poesía
with an expert
not a scribbler.

Will I ever be an expert
at anything?

Poetry, veterinary medicine,
maybe even animal-language
translation?

NOT COMPLETELY BILINGUAL YET

Maybe I should tell la poeta that I know
she's famosa, and maybe we should
switch back to español, instead of
practicing English.

My mouth feels like an acrobat
but I'm determined to learn
    poetry
    words
    English
    everything she can possibly teach me
so I just keep speaking
    push through
as if my tongue
hasn't been tied
into knots.

THE LIBRARY IS A FOREST

Quiet.
Cool.
I search.
Discover.
More.

Baby elephants gain at least
one thousand pounds per year.

La poesía de Gabriela Mistral
y su biografía: she was a teacher
who became the leader of a movement
to change education into a gentle skill
instead of a harsh one, not just
in her own country, but all over
las Américas.

No wonder she loves
    to write
    teach
    work
under the peaceful cover of trees.
The shelves of this library whisper
like fluttering leaves.

CONVERSATION WITH A LIBRARIAN

ME: If you met a famous poet
would you be embarrassed
to show her your first drafts?

HER: No, of course not, writing takes practice
just like any other art—can you imagine
a ballet dancer who goes onstage
without any rehearsals? She would
probably trip
and fall.

ME: I can imagine anything
when I'm writing poetry . . .

HER: Maybe someday
your poems will sit
on these shelves
and I'll be the first
to help someone
find them!

I light up inside.

INVITATION

The next morning
my parents announce
that they'll be even busier than usual,
tending to a pregnant elephant
at the wildlife ranch.

If I promise to be quiet like a library
instead of noisy like a playground,
I can come along and look, without
touching.

INSTRUCTIONS FOR MEETING A
PREGNANT ELEPHANT

Leave dogs and goats at home.
Don't touch ears, or get near feet.

Once she accepts you, she'll always love you
because elephants believe in families,
friendship,
and loyalty.

Never say anything mean or angry
because elephants are so smart
they just might understand you,
so it's better to hum softly
or maybe even sing
a quiet lullaby
for the baby
inside.

ELEPHANT ANATOMY

Standing in front of Chandra
I'm stunned into silence.

Tree-root feet.
Half-moon toenails.
Map-of-India ears.
Paintbrush tail.
A snake-shaped nose
with forty thousand
muscles.

Her fifty-pound heart pulses with love
for her soon-to-be newborn.
She's been pregnant for twenty-two months,
due any day.
She needs to eat three hundred pounds of hay
every twenty-four hours.

When she moves
she's as graceful
as a swaying
ocean wave.

ALL SORTS OF POOP

I've cleaned up almost every variety
of animal scat you can imagine—dog, goat,
cat, weasel, rat, cow, horse, camel, pig,
fish, frog, snake, iguana, and once
the feces of an orphaned sea otter,
the cutest, cuddliest infant
I've ever seen.

But I've never met a real live,
full-sized elefante, with massive
stinky mounds
of greenish waste.

Weird as it sounds
it will be an honor
if my parents let me shovel
these odorous heaps
of digested
wishes.

WHEN ELEPHANTS SING

People listen
   watch
   wait . . .

I find myself trying to translate
every sweet hum, deep rumble,
horselike whinny, birdish chirp,
and lion-powerful
trumpeting
ROAR.

It's language, all of it, including
the silent movements, but is she
asking questions,
or offering answers?

Maybe she's begging
for fencelessness,
an endless forest
for her
   and her soon-to-be-born baby
to freely
explore.

CHANGES

One day with an elephant
is so incredible, so that by the time
I return to my poetry lessons, I finally
have something to write about . . .

only I can't, because the elephant
is too astounding, so all I do is scribble
a few lines, as a half gift
for my teacher.

MY TINY BILINGUAL POEMA
FOR GABRIELA MISTRAL

Poeta y lector
poet and reader

nos conocemos en el aire
we meet in midair

cada palabra
each word

un pájaro
a bird

sin jaula
uncaged,

each phrase

a melody

bright and big

as an elephant.

WILL MY VERSES EVER BE POWERFUL?

It's a fine start, says la poeta.

I set the timid little poem aside.
My future is veterinary science,
not word-strength.

My voice on paper is quiet, not powerful.
I'll just work with animal languages,
like my parents—
learn to understand
    the grunts of gorillas, lowing of bison,
    and chatter of monkeys trained for movies
    about Tarzan, cowboys, and Cleopatra,
    the only woman Hollywood ever shows
    as brave and powerful
train to become
    a courageous animal doctor who saves the most
    ferocious wild creatures
    no matter how dangerous . . .

Maybe they'll make a film about me someday too.

Until then,
I can hope to be friends
with an elephant
and her baby.

BREATH

Once again, I stand before Chandra
spellbound, as if elephants were
wizards.

The elephant's immense height
makes her humming voice sound
like music sent down by the wind
from towering clouds
as she dips her head
and turns to observe me,
with only one curious eye
aimed
at both
of mine.

We stay that way for a long time,
breathing the same air, exchanging
aromas, mine made sweet with candy
and toothpaste, hers a natural storm
of mud, dust, hay bales,
and loneliness.

THE SCENT OF A CAPTIVE ELEPHANT

is solitude

incomplete

exiled

I can smell

her wish to roam

with a herd

family

wildness

THE ELEPHANT'S EYE

Deep
beautiful
darkness

long feathery lashes

peace beyond patience

her eye speaks with stillness
a reminder that humans
are not the only
intelligent
observers
of behavior.

Eye-to-eye
our friendship
is born.

When I blink to see if she'll imitate me,
she winks,
and I know
she really sees me.

ENTRANCED

I float through the next week.

At the clinic, I help Papi heal
a dog that suffered a snakebite.

At the wildlife ranch, Surey lets me
chop fruit to feed Chandra.

All that's missing from my life
is Abuelita, and la isla, the past . . .

but for now, the present
almost feels like
enough.

THE FUTURE IS A QUESTION MARK

I see how my sister looks at Surey.
She's so happy, I can tell
but I can't imagine reaching any age
when romance will be as enchanting
as translating the hums and rumbles
of a nine-thousand-pound
elephant
whose
movements
seem like
fantasies
that are
somehow

real.

THE PRESENT IS WINGED

I feel
like I'm flying
back and forth
between worlds—
home, clinic, library,
wildlife ranch
   and poetry
    trees.

There's no telling where
my thoughts will end up
by the end of the day
when I'm sleeping
and dreams
emerge . . .

ELEPHANTS HEAR WITH THEIR FEET

Sometimes dreams are easier
to believe than truth.

From Surey, I learn
that the soles of huge feet
absorb distant vibrations.

In the wild forests of Nepal,
Chandra would be able to tell
when another herd was approaching.

Now, imagine how scary it must sound
to the skin of her feet, as they listen
to the ground, whenever a movie star's
fancy sports car roars uphill
with visitors from Hollywood.

People whose faces I recognize from movies
point, wave, shout, and demand answers,
even though Surey tells them he's not sure
exactly when the baby is due.

Cat says he does know,
but he doesn't want anyone
annoying the sensitive elephant
at the moment when she gives birth

to a creature that will only
   need
   want
its own mother's
humming
voice.

VOICES

Wherever I go
I keep thinking
about those hums
and the listening feet,
and my own dog and goat,
and the birdsongs of Cuba,
and every other sound
that can turn into
a poem.

And I wonder
if every person
has a sound
   a poem
inside them too.

WHEN I SET MY MUSICAL
MEMORIES FREE

In Cuba, the little blue birds called azulitos
sang *breep-breep-too-to-too-wee.*
Bijiritas whistled exactly seven notes,
and sinsontes improvised,
copying another bird's melody,
then changing it into
a completely new
invention.

So that's what I try
each time I scribble verses
in the shadow of Gabriela Mistral
and her trees.

Some of my poemas
sink deep into dark soil
with hidden
roots

but others
rise like wings.

THE POET'S STORIES ARE RIDDLES

Gabriela says that when she was a little girl
she thought trees were enchanted boys,
so she spoke to them, but a few years later
she grew up and realized that forests
are more like parents
with strong hands
that lift
    carry
    pass humans
from branch
to branch,
holding us up.

MY STORIES ARE NEVER FINISHED . . .

so instead of trying to scribble
I introduce Gabriela Mistral
and Doris
to my parents
    my sister
    Surey
    and Chandra

it's a day of clear sky
fluffy clouds

everyone accepts
the two women who look
like they long to hold hands
and the elephant who seems
to be whooshing her breath
out through her trunk
as if sending messages
far across the sea
to the green foothills
of the Himalayas

ELEPHANT SERENADE

Mud.
A pond.
The slime
of green algae.

She rolls in sludge,
sprays with her trunk,
coats herself, and then
rises up out of the muck
and steps forward
to greet us.

I brush
the delicate tip of her mouth
with my fingers.

La poeta does the same, and soon
we are all humming an elephant song
composed by the animal herself.

SINGER

The next morning
poetry flows like a waterfall
cascading
so
maybe
I do
have
my
own
word
song
after
all.

OBSERVER

On the day when we all sang together
I noticed how my parents accepted Gabriela Mistral
just as naturally as if she were not world-famous,
thanking her for taking the time to help me improve
my writing skills.

Now, two days later, all I can think about
is the way poetry is growing inside of me,
and how closely I need to watch
Chandra
if I'm ever
going to write
about her . . .

LISTENER

If there is one thing I've learned
from Gabriela Mistral, it's the art
of keeping my ears open to the
    sounds of nature
    stories of life
that surround us,
that make us who we are.

She speaks
to me
about the cruelty
    she experienced as a child—
    the teacher who
called her stupid
    accused her
    of stealing notebooks
then made her
stand out in the street, where other niños
were told to throw sharp stones at her
until she fell down,
bleeding.

WHY?

It's the question
even famous poets
can't seem to answer.

Why would a teacher
choose to be so cruel?

Why would children
choose to obey such a vicious command?

¿Por qué?
La poeta famosa
still has no answer,
even after so many years.

A better question, she suggests, is how
can you and I avoid becoming cruel too?
We must work hard,
    be like the elephant,
aware of our strength,
yet gentle to others,
kind to ourselves.

HOW TO RAISE AN ELEPHANT BABY

The next time I try to write a poem,
I'm in the elephant barn
watching Chandra
and wondering
if she knows
that in the wild
she would have been
surrounded by aunties,
all the female elephants
of a herd, determined
to help care for her baby.

Their songs of togetherness
would have sounded like the hums
she is releasing right now, only
multiplied:
hmmmmmmm
HMMMMMMMM
HAAAAAAAAAAA
in many voices, a chorus
of contentment
   love
   support.

EAGER

The poet has only visited Chandra once
because she's busy
with la poesía
and diplomacy,
but I return every day
with Flora and Fauna
all of us walk, walk, walking
uphill to sing and dance,
play, run, splash,
with the pregnant elephant
whose name means *moon*.

I can hardly wait to see
the baby, and learn his name—
or hers—Star, Comet, Meteor,
Planet?

WORDLESS

Each time we make eye contact
I feel like I'm slowly learning
to translate
this elephant's hums
and rumbles.

Words aren't the only way
to turn life into a poem
that almost
rhymes.

Imagine if I turn out to be
the world's first animal-language
interpreter, sought out by zoos
and circuses
all over the world
just to tell trainers what they
already know in their hearts,
that elephants love music
and need humming
herds.

A FABLE ABOUT AN
ELEPHANT'S SECRET

Today, instead of a poetry lesson,
Gabriela Mistral writes a fable and reads it
out loud.

The tale begins with a mountain's shadow.
An elephant emerges from the shade.
He has no eyes, so he wishes, wishes,
wishes, until finally, he can see.
Then he grows tusks
made of moonlight
and he realizes
that all the other
animals in the jungle
are terrified
by his size,
so he sets out
to prove that he
is kind, not cruel.

The elephant helps each animal
whenever he sees that it needs
his strength.

He rescues a baby monkey
that is trapped on a high branch.

He uses his long trunk
to swish flies away
from a giraffe's back.

He frees a rhino
that is wedged
between two
trees.

Soon, all the animals know
that the elephant is kind,
not cruel.

He never tells them the secret
of his origin, how he slowly walked
out of the shadow
of a mountain,
but his kindness
speaks for itself.

I hope I can learn to write verses
that show how people-like creatures
can grow more and more
friendly.

SHADOWY

The fable
seems shaded
by dark and light
meanings.

I'm not sure why the elephant
has to keep his mountainous nature
secret.

Am I part shadow too,
and part wish, and part
moonlight?

Every time I meet someone new
will I have to show that I can be a friend
even though at first we'll feel
like strangers?

TREETOPS

Sometimes my happy pattern
of visiting Chandra, working
at the clinic, listening to la poeta
and scribbling under trees
is interrupted by Gabriela Mistral's
job as a diplomat
when she must travel,
    receive grown-up visitors
    give speeches
        at conferences
        and universities.

Fancy cars park in front of her house.
Fancy men and ladies carry books
for her to sign,
documents for her
to approve.

There are weeks when she is
overseas, in some distant land, at a gala—
a ceremony in her honor.

Those are the moments I choose
for climbing trees in her garden

When I miss her
the leaves carry her voice
as they
whisper and whistle
like songbirds
in Cuba.

ODE TO MY POETRY TEACHER

courage
is a dance of words
on paper
as graceful as an elephant
the size of love

gracias
thank you
for metaphors
and similes
vowel rhymes
counted lines
and flowing ones
free verse
and formal
wild
natural
musical
me

MYSTERY

When la poeta returns
from one of her journeys
she reads what I've written
and begins to weep.

Juan Miguel, she murmurs,
before disappearing into her house
as if it were a cave, her suitcase
abandoned
beside the door.

I'm left with the feeling
that the verses I scribbled
are not as happy-ever-after
as I had imagined.

Who is Juan Miguel,
and why does he make
the poet cry?

TRAGEDY

While la poeta rests,
Doris comes out of the house
and quietly explains
that Gabriela Mistral
had a son, either her own
or an adopted nephew,
no one but the poet
knows for sure.

Together, Gabriela and Juan Miguel
lived in Brazil—he was a teenager,
it was only two years ago.
The Brazilian town was a lovely one,
but some of the boys Juan Miguel's age
and a little older
envied his talent
for studying,
resented
his mother's fame,
hated him
for being a foreigner,
mocked him
for being a bit different—
just slightly hunchbacked
as if he'd been injured
at birth, born twisted.

So they killed him, Doris states calmly.
The police refused to investigate
simply because Juan Miguel
was an outsider, and they
were xenophobic.

Gabriela felt certain that her boy
was poisoned, but she could not
convince the officials.

They ordered her to accept their decision
to call it an accident, or a natural death
due to too much rum, but Juan Miguel
was not a drinker,
he was just a boy—
sweet, shy,
homesick
from another country.

XENOPHOBIA

I leave Doris and walk to the library,
find a massive dictionary,
flip through the heavy pages,
and look up the word:
xenophobic.

Xeno means outsider.
Phobia is fear.

The boys who killed Gabriela Mistral's son
were afraid of outsiders—that's why they
hated him, because the line between
fear
and hate
is a wavy one
that flows back and forth
like water
or air.

How strange it seems
that one can turn into the other.

But if fear can become hatred,
then maybe courage
can transform
into friendship . . .

It's the sort of thing I would have asked
Abuelita when she was alive, or la poeta
if she weren't grieving.

For now
all I can do is carry the question
around inside me,
because I don't want
to bother my parents
while they're working
or my sister when she's
busy flirting.

I'll just tuck xenophobia
into a suitcase full of
confusion, and take it out
later, when someone wiser
can help me send it
far away.

THE POET'S SUITCASE

The very next day
I see the poet's luggage
still abandoned beside her door.

We'll have to move soon,
Doris explains gently.
All diplomats
are required
to go
wherever
peace between nations
is threatened, and peacemakers
of the poetic sort
might be able
to help.

I hear the words
but they make no sense—

My teacher
    la poeta
    my friend
is leaving?

WAVE AFTER WAVE

Peace is always threatened—
by
bullies.
Murderers.
Xenophobes.
War.
Moving away . . .

The lives of adults are so complicated
that I almost wish I could be a child
forever.

La poeta
and the elephant help me feel whole
in an odd way that gives me
twinges of guilt,
because for the first time I realize—
though
I still love Abuelita
and Cuba
as much as ever,
I no longer
yearn for them
every moment
of every day.

ANGRY

More than guilty,
I'm mad.
Mad at those bullies
who killed Juan Miguel,
and I'm furious
with Gabriela Mistral
for being a diplomat
who needs to move away
someday, sooner or later,
just because she's a peacemaker,
as if being una poeta famosa
were not enough.

So I walk uphill alone
to recite my rhymes out loud
to Chandra, who does not care
if I'm stupid, or speak
with an accent.

All she longs for
are her elephant baby
and elephant aunties
to help her raise Star
or Comet
or Meteor
or Planet . . .

OUT LOUD

Hand in trunk with the elephant,
I recite poems, and together
we sway as if dancing,
not mourning.

Elephants seem to understand
the part of poetry that has no words
just music that echoes
like wind chimes
or bells.

AFTER A TRAGEDY

Just like Juan Gabriel
and Abuelita,
some of the patients
at our veterinary clinic
don't survive
when sickness or tragedy
strikes.

Only a few hours after my solitary
walk along the beach, an old dog
that was hit by a car
floats
up to the sky
where Abuelita surely needs
a canine companion.

While my parents try to comfort the owner,
my own mind soars toward Flora and Fauna,
the pets I know best, the animals I cuddle,
groom, feed, and play with every day.
How would I feel if they . . .
but no—for now they're safe
so I tell myself to be brave
and celebrate.

RONDA

That night, instead of wishing
that things were different, I read
some of Gabriela Mistral's rondas—
rhymed poems that were written
for children who feel like dancing.

Each ronda has lines of seven syllables
repeated four times, with rhymes—
or words that almost rhyme—at the ends
of alternate lines.

I try
to scribble
a little ronda
of my own:
From happiness to sorrow
and back again in circles
we dance until tomorrow
with dazzling leaps and twirls.

Soon I'm on my feet with Flora and Fauna,
all three of us performing a clumsy ballet
of paws, hooves, and bedroom slippers,
as we spin
round
and round,

transforming
most of my sadness
into a single
moment
of hope.

Grief and joy
have a way
of taking turns
in the vast
spinning
galaxy
of verses.

AN ELEPHANT BABY WILL
BE BORN TODAY!

Finally, the evening
I've been waiting for arrives,
but when labor starts, my parents
refuse to let me help, or even
observe.

They tell me that if anything goes wrong
it will upset me so much more than the loss
of that poor old dog.

But they don't understand—
how will I ever be a veterinarian
if I don't learn to tolerate
blood
and pain?

I defy clear instructions
for the first time
in my life.

I need to witness the birth of this baby.

SPYING

Alone
I leave home
to zigzag my way
through neighbors' yards
instead of staying on streets,
so that I won't be visible
or punishable.

Finally,
I reach the ranch and
sneak up to the elephant barn.
If Mima and Papi catch me
they'll make Cat babysit me
as if I were still just una niñita
with no common sense.

From a small window
on one wall of the enormous
barn
I peek in, ready to watch
a marvel, a wondrous,
unimaginable
milagro
but sometimes
miracles take time.

Right now
all I see is agony
and the horror
of uncertainty . . .

AN ELEPHANT'S ORDEAL

Chandra lies down, stands, kneels,
collapses, rolls, rises, groans, then shoves
her entire mountain-shadow body
against the wall
where I peer
through the window
like a tiny
mouse.

Minutes pass.
Hours?
How can something
as ancient and natural as birth
turn out to be so challenging
to watch?

NATURAL WONDERS

Finally,
a baby elephant
slips to the ground,
enclosed in a sac
that looks like
wet silk.

But then . . .
another
soon
follows.

Twins!

SUSPICIOUS

From outside, at the window,
I hear cheering from
   my parents
   Surey
   Cat
and a man whose voice
is so familiar
that the sound
seems eerie.

Someone famous? An actor?
From all those corny
cowboy movies?

What is he doing here
right at this moment?

ELEPHANT NEEDS

Twin elephants are rare.

What Chandra needs right now is
   calm
   comfort
   health for her babies . . .
not a visit from a famous stranger.

What does he want?
Will my parents be able to prevent
the actor from inviting all his friends
to meet the newborns?

SHUT UP, CREEP

As the actor goes on and on
in his familiar silver screen voice
where everything sounds magnified,
I breathe three deep sighs
of relief,
one for each
of the elephants.

Shut up, I grumble, but of course
the actor inside the barn can't hear me,
so I leave, sneak back home, and climb
into bed without wishing or whistling.
I just whisper one quick little
gracias a Dios prayer for radiance,
because dar a luz—to give to the light—
is the Cuban way
of saying
to give birth,
and it has never seemed
more true than now
with the moon
flooding my room
as if Flora and Fauna
and I are all
orbiting flecks

of space dust
in a universe
of darkness
y luz.

DREAMS OF HUMMING

Chandra's language comes back
while I'm asleep, all the *hmmmms*
that sounded as if she were
pleading with the air
to transform
her pain
into music.

New life
from ancient,
she seemed to announce
inside the dream world
where words
are not needed.

FAMILIA AND OTHER QUESTIONS

In the morning, I want to tell
Gabriela Mistral
that the babies were born,
but I realize—
I didn't stay at the barn
long enough to find out
whether the twins
are boys or girls.

Do they have names yet?
Will the elephant family
be happy without a herd
of helpful aunties?

Are my parents home?
And what about Cat—
will she tell me whatever
she knows about why
the loudmouth actor
was lurking and shouting
where he was not wanted?

NO ONE IS HOME

So I do all my chores,
feed the animals
   clean cages
   and then walk
back uphill
to the elephant barn
where Chandra is brushing
one baby with her trunk
while the other nurses
under her belly.

Mima and Papi are gone.
Only Surey and my sister
are here.

Cat gazes at her boyfriend
instead of the babies.

She's in love, or someplace
in between fantasies
and plans.

TWIN ELEPHANTS

Heart, limbs, pulse, skin,
I can hardly believe how much
the babies grew
while they remained hidden
inside their mamá.

Now that they're here,
I long to choose suitable names,
even though it's not really my job; they have
an owner—either the wildlife ranch
or, as Cat claims with disgust, the actor
whose noisy voice annoyed me so much
last night.

Why would the actor choose
their names? I ask her.

They were sold, my sister says.

WHERE TO NEXT

What?
This makes no sense.

Surey shakes his head and adds,
We don't even know if they'll stay here
or go somewhere else,
and wherever
Chandra lives, I've always
gone with her—we are
a two-species
herd.

First Gabriela Mistral
says she must leave.
Now Surey and Chandra might too?

NO

I know what it means
to leave
to go somewhere new.

But sold?
SOLD??

How can someone
put a price on
   make property of
creatures as amazing
as elephants?

No, no, no, no, no.

They need names,
they do not need
to be moved away
to a private estate
or . . .

Wait.

Why is the actor so interested
in Chandra in the first place?

Is he preparing for a safari movie?
With Chandra as his huge
sidekick—one of those silly
unscientific films
where orangutans
are shown in Egypt
instead of Borneo
where they
belong?

Is the actor taking Chandra
to a movie studio?

THE NAMES OF PAIRS

I stand as close to Chandra
as Surey recommends, just close enough
to make eye contact, but not so near
that she'll be fearful, or feel the need
to protect her babies.

My sister starts reciting paired names
that could be suitable for one boy
and one girl,
based on the examination
made by my parents.

Jacob and Esau in Israel, Cat says,
but those were both boy twins.

Apollo and Artemis in Greece,
she continues, Romulus and Remus
in Rome . . .

But again those were male
Star and Planet, I say.
Comet and Meteor.

I think about Chandra's humming.
The music she makes naturally.

What about
Song and Dance?

Those are the perfect names!
No one sways more rhythmically
than an elephant.

TROUBLE

At first both babies have wobbly legs
and pinkish bellies, wide eyes, clumsy trunks,
and open mouths, but by the time Song,
the sweet male, and Dance, the lively female,
are one whole week old, reporters,
movie producers, and famous Hollywood stars
begin to arrive in excited clusters, cameras
flashing
like fireworks,
questions bellowed
at the noise level of roaring trains,
absurdly posed safari photos staged
with props from Kenya
instead of Nepal—can't newspaper
photographers tell the difference
between African elephants
and Asian?

Everything feels frantic
and frenzied in this place
that is usually
so peaceful.

REFUGE

My parents are worried.
Fame is not one of the situations
an elephant mother craves
for her babies.

Unable to relax, Song and Dance
hide behind Chandra, as if she really is
a beautiful, boulder-clad mountain
with a cool, soothing
blue-gray
shadow.

Elephants are smart—
they feel the frenzy too.

CONVERSATION WITH
AN ELEPHANT FAMILY

ME: Don't worry.

BABIES: *hmmmmmm*
HMMMMMMMM

CHANDRA: *HAAAAAAAAAAAAAAA*

ME: Your voices feel like
musical hugs.

I tell Chandra I'll help
the elephants.
I won't let anyone
disturb them, or create
more and more chaos
where there should be
peace.

CATASTROPHE

My promise fails
the very next day.

Without any warning,
one of the babies
vanishes.

Dance is gone.
Stolen?
Kidnapped?

Not just traded to a zoo or circus,
but actually hidden by the actor
whose boasting
makes me so furious.

He's there, in the elephant barn,
bragging to my parents
about his wilderness skills
and experience training
dangerous beasts.
Mima argues.
Papi fumes.
Cat and Surey
stand quietly
listening.

Is there nothing we can do
to change a brute's mind?

Song is frantic,
and Chandra infuriated,
both of them charging
in and out of the barn
all over the pasture
    searching
    searching
    searching . . .

THIEF

The actor won't say why he moved
one baby and not the other.

He shrugs, grins, mentions something about
a fascinating project, a filmmaking experiment
that will thrill every kid who loves movies . . .

We need to know where that baby is now,
Mima states calmly, but forcefully, using
the tone she reserves for cruel people
who abuse animals.

A newborn needs its mother's milk, Papi
explains, and closeness, contact, touch . . .

The sound of her hum, I want to add,
but my voice refuses to burst from
my mouth, I'm so upset that I'm silent
like clouds before
a hurricane.

GUILT

I should have stood guard
all day and all night, protecting
the most trusting animal family
I've ever met.

How can creatures
so enormous
and intelligent
be so vulnerable?

I gaze up at Chandra:
We'll find Dance, I say,
she belongs with you,
we'll bring her back,
I won't
let her be taken away
ever again . . .

and I pray that
this
is a promise
I can keep.

SINGING OUR SORROWS

I stand with Song
shoulder to shoulder
both of us swaying
like trees in a breeze.

Hand to trunk
breath to breath
we hum
and hope,
each syllable
of *hmmm*
hmm
hmm
bringing me
a bit closer
to understanding
his grief.

GRIEF

This is how I felt when Abuelita
died from diabetes, even after we'd
moved from one country to another
in search of experts and research . . .

This is how I felt when mean kids
called me zoo beast, and a teacher
thought I was stupid, and a glass
statuette on my windowsill
was not enough to change
the future.

I know what Gabriela Mistral
would say, even without asking—
put your sadness into a poem,
there is no better home
for emotions.

SIZE

I try to write.

But this wave of sadness towers
like the ocean during hurricanes.

I can't find any way to shrink it
into a little verse in either language,
the one from my homeland,
or this new set of English words
with no predictable rules
for pronunciation.

The wave of anger grows
                    moves
from my heart to my mind.

It won't fit in a poem,
so I must speak in
Chandra's language
of rumbles
and roars . . .

STARLIGHT

I sneak out alone
without Flora and Fauna
to visit la poeta
in darkness.

I've never entered
her garden
at night.

I expect to find her indoors, reading,
but instead, she and Doris are outside
gazing up at the stars,
holding hands.

When I ask her advice, she says
Write letters to everyone who might care,
anyone who might know if there are rules
governing the complicated realm of kindness
to las bestiecitas.

KINDNESS TO ANIMALS

I imagine it as a vast realm
like the night sky, with no visible center,

galaxies that glow
when you look up at constellations.

They have names
and faces
   histories
   stories
that vary
from one country
to another.

I imagine it as a place where animals wait
to be recognized as more
than metaphors.

Will letters really be enough
to change the minds of people
who don't even care about kindness
to one another?

BLAZE

I've never liked cowboy movies,
except for the horses and cattle,
so I don't remember the obnoxious
actor's name, until I look it up
in a magazine at the library.

Blaze.
Just one word.
No surname.

I guess it's supposed to
make him seem heroic
but in my opinion
he's a villain—
in films
he always kills
Comanches, Apaches,
and mexicanos
who are just trying
to protect their land
from thieves.

LIBRARIES AREN'T ALWAYS
PERFECTLY QUIET

When I do a little more research,
I discover that the name Blaze is from
the Latin root *blaesus*, meaning stammering.

I gasp, which brings the librarian
rushing to join me, but she also smiles kindly
so I know she's not really mad, just worried
about the old folks around me, who expect
libraries to be as solemn
as cemeteries.

Modern librarians
love fun and happiness,
not silence.

LETTERS

The next time I visit her,
Gabriela Mistral says letters
may not be enough.
She says I need
to write pleas for the reunification
of the separated elephant family.

Writing, she insists, has always been
a form of embrace, a hug that lets people know
you care about their opinions, and their joy,
sorrows, efforts—above all, their hopes.
Writing can change
the world.

She writes letters to her poet friends
every single day, without fail.

When I ask why, she lists poets
who are already famous: Pablo Neruda
in Chile, and Langston Hughes, who is from
the US, but has lived in Mexico
and traveled in Cuba.

She writes to encourage them
even though they no longer need praise.
She writes because letters are the best way

to say that she loves their work, and hopes
they know she supports them.

She writes to women poets too,
even though she says their names
are not as well-known: Victoria Ocampo
from Argentina, Juana de Ibarbourou
in Uruguay, and others who are timid
and need so much encouragement
that Gabriela Mistral's letters
often begin with Dear Silent Poet
or Dear Ferocious Poet,
to let them know that they need
to write, write, write . . .

She reminds me that I am
a Silent Poet
whenever I do not
scribble, scribble, scribble,
and that whenever she moves away
I must send her examples of my verses
as I practice, practice, practice,
if I want to become a Ferocious Poet
on paper
too.

NOT ENOUGH PRACTICE

I practice
and practice
but I don't know how
to make my letters stronger.
They are not ferocious.
They're weak little creatures
that won't change anyone's mind.

For now, Mima
promises to write to the Humane
Association, and Papi says he
will call other veterinarians
and zoology professors
who might know some way
to take the actor to court
and force him to be kind
instead of cruel.

COMFORTING A HEARTBROKEN
MOTHER AND BROTHER

With grown-ups writing the letters,
I spend my time consoling
Chandra, talking, stroking, humming,
and playing games with Song:
elephant mud tag, where we roll
and then chase each other,
elephant soccer, kicking a ball
with our feet and heads,
or in Song's case, his trunk,
an advantage that allows him
to always win.

The tip of his trunk is still uncoordinated,
so while Chandra picks up tiny peanuts,
Song brushes his nose in mud, then paints
a brown landscape of smudges
on my face.

MOVEMENT

The beauty of elephants
makes me cry, sigh, smile,
as they sway with sorrow,
wave their ears,
and lift their voices
to hug me
with hums.

Hmmmm,
I reply,
trying to explain
that I'll be back tomorrow.
Right now I need to go out
searching.

A DOG'S NOSE

Flora helps me.
Her sense of smell
is a form of intelligence.

She's found Fauna
so many times
that all I have to do
is let her smell one
of the twin elephants,
then pronounce
the command FIND
in such a firm way
that she knows
I'm serious.

This is work.
She becomes a hound
hunting wolves, recovers
her ancient energy
for pursuing prey,
only of course
she's tame
and would never
hurt anyone.

She races
ahead of me,
leading me
swiftly
with certainty
past dozens and dozens
of baby elephant
footprints.

Poor Dance must be exhausted
after walking so far!

Lucky for me, she was led,
not trucked, because that means
she can't be too far away . . .
Can she?

EVERYTHING IS HIDDEN

Bamboo,
a towering
impenetrable
curtain of stems.

If only I could grow wings
and soar above this thicket
to spy from above
and discover
Dance.

Flora leads, I follow, and finally,
when she spins around to show me
her excited eyes and wagging tail, I know
we must be making progress.

We emerge with leaf-scratched faces
and dusty skin, but beyond the bamboo
we find a corral, and inside, there's a boy
around my age, feeding a little elephant
with the world's biggest
baby bottle.

DISCOVERY

I step out of the shadowy cover of bamboo
with my hand on Flora's head, to keep her
from greeting Dance too boisterously,
or scaring the strange boy.

Not that I plan to be friendly myself,
just direct and abrupt, as I tell the kid
that he's feeding a baby who belongs
with her mother and twin, not him.

His response astonishes me: You mean
she's not an orphan, like Blaze said?

I shake my head fiercely,
too shocked to answer
in words.

LIAR

Blaze lied! the boy howls,
making me gasp
with a mixture of relief
and excitement,
because maybe I'm not
the only one
who hates Blaze enough now
to defy him.

He always lies, I state firmly,
even though I don't really know
if it's completely true, but that is,
after all, exactly what actors do,
isn't it—Blaze makes a living
pretending to be brave,
using words that aren't his,
while behind the scenes
he's a coward, thief, liar,
and probably the world's
most vicious
animal
tormentor . . .

CONVERSATION WITH CARLITOS

ME: Who are you? Will you help me return
this baby to her mother and twin brother?
All we have to do is open the gate and lead her
out of the bamboo, over a few hills
to safety.

HIM: I'm Carlos like my Papi, but he
calls me Carlitos—he's a horse trainer,
but Blaze hired him to teach
this little elephant
how to talk.
      Who are you?

ME: Oriol, well, Olivia, but Oriol too—
what do you mean teach him to
talk?

HIM: Blaze says lonely elephants get so bored
that they can learn to imitate
human voices.
Just like parrots
and macaws . . .

I'M TOO STUNNED TO SPEAK

Macaws mate for life.
They need to be free.
Parrots too.
No bird would ever mimic
human words,
a language not their own,
unless
it was tortured
with the sheer
boredom
of isolation.

CARLITOS EXPLAINS

Blaze says a baby elephant
can be taught to grab its tongue
with its trunk, twist it around,
and make a sound
that is almost
HELLO.

I shake my head,
close my eyes tight.
What would Gabriela Mistral say
if she knew language was being used
for torture?

I release my grip on Flora,
let go so she can leap
over the fence of the corral
to play
with Dance,
her reward
for a successful
search.

SEARCH AND RESCUE

Finding a lost victim is never enough.
We need to rescue Dance too, lead her
away from this nightmare.

Ayúdame, I plead, but Carlitos
does not understand Spanish.

He says he was born in Los Angeles,
and his family has lived in California
for hundreds of years, long before
it was seized during a war, forced
to become part of the US.

I don't know enough local history
to make sense of this, but I do know
that Dance can't survive
the torture
of loneliness.

Help me, I translate, and quietly,
gently, like a trainer who cares
about the animal he tends,
Carlitos says,
Yes, of course,

I'll help
the stolen baby.
But how do we
start?

ISOLATION

Alone.
So alone.
I stroke
Dance's head,
ears, face, trunk.

She wraps her long nose
around my arm, grasps my hand,
helps me learn how to feed her
with the giant baby bottle.

Goat's milk and formula,
Carlitos explains, not ideal
but better than nothing,
and she needs to nurse
for two whole years.

Let's open the gate
and lead her home,
I suggest, she doesn't
need to be isolated,
there's no reason
for her to learn
stupid tricks
like pronouncing
a human word,

separation
from her family
is a torment
for all of them,
but we're free
to free her,
just pretend
you never saw me,
I'll lead her
to her mama
and hermanito
on my own.

IMPRISONED

Carlitos agrees—
his father is asleep
because he guards Dance
during the night shift,
and Carlitos feeds her
in the daytime,
but he doesn't
have the key
to a gate
that was locked
by Blaze himself.

Dance
is a prisoner,
and we are just two
of the few people who know
where she is
and why.

FRIENDS?

Together, Carlitos and I watch
as Flora and Dance play tag,
peekaboo,
and elephant
acrobatic games,
rambling in circles
then stopping
suddenly,
so dizzy
that both
wobble
and
almost
fall . . .

LAUGHTER IS AN OPEN GATE

Carlitos and I face
a complicated dilemma—
how can we rescue an animal
that others have already claimed?—
but as we watch animals
of different species
play together so easily,
everything else
seems possible too.

All we have to do
is belong to a team
of people who care
about kindness,
and find a way
to be
brave.

SINGING SESSION WITH A CANINE

Flora and I walk home
happily, sadly, hopefully,
and musically, listening
to our footsteps
as we thump
stomp
and bark-chant
    what's next
    what now
    what if
we try this plan . . .
or that one . . .
or something
else?

PLANNING SESSION WITH HUMANS

I start with grown-ups.
Mima and Papi are shocked,
but they warn me not to cut the lock
with any of their garden tools, they could
end up in jail for stealing a legally
purchased
animal.

Gabriela Mistral once again suggests
written appeals, but this time she says
it could be a petition, instead of letters,
I could gather many signatures
of people who will demand
justice for Dance
and Song
and Chandra.

PLANNING SESSION WITH ELEPHANTS

I tell Chandra
that I found Dance.

She trumpets.
Does she understand?

I tell Song.
He rumbles.
Hums.
Chirps.
Swipes at my braid
with his trunk, and tugs it
playfully, but he's strong
so it hurts, and for just
one moment, I wonder
if he knows that his strength
is amazing.

We'll figure it out, I promise,
standing off to one side
at a safe distance.

HOW TO WRITE A PETITION
FOR JUSTICE

Scribble, tear it up, try again,
and again, each lost page
just a shadow
of something
I meant
to say.

Exhausted and frustrated,
I recall a time when Gabriela Mistral told me
that she's writing a long ghost poem, words
that won't
be read by anyone
until she's invisible,
floating like air.

Write from your blood, she advised me.
Write from your tree sap, your spirit,
your heart, roots, breath.

So I try again and again,
switching to poesía,
with or without rhyme,
counting syllables,
letting the rhythm
flow naturally, then I try

once more, and once more,
until finally, the last page
seems to speak in a voice
that is not
my own
but is also fully mine.

PETITION FROM A FAMILY

We need
to be together,
a trumpeting herd
forever.

We plead to be united.
Your help is really needed.

Imagine you in our place,
so cruelly separated.

Please speak
and seek sweet justice.

Signed with the tips of our trunks
dipped in mud:
Chandra
Song
Dance.

THE FIRST SIGNATURES

mud
trunks
squiggles
scribbles
try again
keep trying
there it is
an initial
for each:
C
S
D

Who needs whole names anyway?
These are the pen names
of elephant
poets.

THE NEXT SIGNATURES

. . . are people I know, first the grown-ups,
then Cat, Surey, and Carlitos,
who offers to walk with me door
to door, asking neighbors
and strangers
to join
our campaign
for elephant justice,
a heartfelt goal
that might not ever
be in our control, but at least
we haven't given up.

WHAT IF?

What if we fail?
What if no one cares?

What if this first house
is the home of some fanatic
fan of Blaze, who will surely
rage against us when he
finds out that we've
organized a plan
to defeat a villain
who happens to be
    famous
     popular
     and rich?

SLOW PROGRESS

The Humane Association promises
to send a delegation to investigate,
but Mima and Papi warn me
that they can't work quickly,
because laws are complicated,
and we don't want trouble
of the sort that could
get us deported . . .

so in the meantime, I keep walking,
walking, walking, up and down hills
all over town, accompanied by my dog,
my goat, and a new friend—Carlitos,
whose father has agreed to let him
take this time off, because both of them
were tricked by Blaze, and now they
don't want to be the cause
of any more suffering
for anyone.

NEIGHBORHOODS

Some people treat us like we're
dangerous, while others step outside
and chat with us, or invite us in
for milk and cookies
    shake their heads
    offer sympathy
for the elephant mother
and her babies.

At one house,
the door opens on
a girl
    Alice
who teased me
at school last year.

She says she's never been allowed
to have a pet.
What's it like to live with so many
animals? she asks.

I like it. Animals don't judge,
I say.

I'm sorry for making
fun of you, she says.

I smile.
Wanna help us?

FRIENDSHIP

Carlitos and Alice
both walk with me, collecting
more and more signatures.

Then we sit down at my kitchen table
and we all write letters to movie stars,
studios, directors, producers,
Hollywood script writers.

Gabriela Mistral has promised to mail them.
She says she and Doris can find any address
at the library.

So now we wait.
It's easy.
All we have to do is talk, talk, talk,
and play with Flora, Fauna, and any other
animal that happens to need exercise
right here at our clinic, where kindness
is sometimes as simple as spending time
chopping carrots for a porcupine,
or washing lettuce for rabbits.

BELONGING

Here I am
both with an accent
and speaking fluently

making friends with creatures
and people

learning animal music
and poetry.

I feel as though I belong here
like towering mountains
and their shadows.

AT THE END OF EACH DAY

I visit the lonely baby.
We still need to rescue her,
but until that happens, I feel encouraged
by the simple togetherness
of friendship.

I don't know where Blaze is
or how to defy him, but for now
all I know is how to share
companionship.

Carlitos and his kindhearted papi
let Dance play with Flora and Fauna,
who both love to cuddle, hum-hug,
trumpet-chase, and just generally
embrace us with music
and movements
that resemble
a round-and-round
ronda of verses.

CHILDREN AND ANIMALS
BELONG TOGETHER

Carlitos and Alice cheer
when Flora, Fauna, and Dance
begin to play tag, then they lunge
into the game, yell at me to join,
shout You're it, and let me win just once
before we all begin to play seriously,
each of us chasing the dog, goat,
and baby elephant in circles,
all of us
stumbling
and giggling
as we risk
being trampled . . .

but the game is so much fun
that we just keep going round
and round in circles
until, exhausted,
Dance stops
and hugs
each of us
with a *hmmmmmmm*.

IN PRAISE OF HUMMING

Hmmm is a question and answer
at the same time, *hmmmmmmm*
is a language shared by many species,
not just pachyderms,
but purring felines,
sighing canines,
the whirring wings
of avians,
and buzzing
thrum of bees.

Hmmm
can even be
a song
sung
by trees
in a breeze.

Hmmm
can also be a plea
for help.

A sound that says
Thank you for being here.
A sound that says
I'm lonely.

When I look at Dance
I hear her *hmmm* all three.
And I know she needs me
to reunite the divided family.

When I sing *hmmmmm*
back, it's a promise:
Yes, I will.

ELEPHANT INTELLIGENCE

Each time I return to Chandra
she sniffs my hands, as if she knows
where I've been
and whose soft gray skin
I've touched.

She's so smart that she makes tools
by stripping leaves off a branch
to create her own flyswatter,
and she teases Surey, covering his head
with a hat made of hay, then nibbling
one strand at a time.

Elephants are so intelligent
that I feel certain Chandra,
Song,
and Dance
must all know how hard
we're trying
to reunite them.

FLOATING

One day, just when I'm feeling
impatient and discouraged, as I wait
for more answers to my letters,
Chandra wraps her trunk around me
and lifts me onto her shoulders
where I drift like a cloud—
my
mind
weightless.

Only my body feels real,
both solid and fragile,
but my worries
are gone, at least
in this moment.

This is an entirely different sort of hug,
one made of height, and hope,
and the luck that floats
in every breath
of air.

BACK ON EARTH

We have a three-way staring contest.
Chandra's eyes are dark and deep
like midnight.

Song still has flecks of pink
around his eyelids, surrounded
by smoky gray skin
with silvery highlights
and lavender shadows.

Baby elephants look as vulnerable
as newborn birds without feathers.

Even more vulnerable
when they're alone.

RESONANCE

Surey tells me
that in Kathmandu,
every Nepali who touches
an elephant
feels blessed.

It's like an echo
that vibrates
for an entire
lifetime.

Is that why
I feel a buzzing within me
when I think of
rescuing Dance?

ANSWERS ARRIVE

At first it's just a trickle,
then a river of letters
pledging help
    encouragement
    support
and above all
words, words, words
that we can quote
over and over—words
from people so famous
that no newspaper would dream
of ignoring their statements.

Phrases condemning an atrocity
against innocent animals
are followed by vows
to write letters
directly
to
Blaze!

AN ENTIRE LIFETIME

That's the image I carry with me
as I finally set out to confront
the elephant tormentor
who calls himself Blaze
because he doesn't
know its meaning,
and he's probably
never wondered
about the difference
between language
and mimicry either,
and he definitely does not
understand that isolation in childhood
can cause a lifetime of loneliness
unless someone else steps in
to challenge
and demand
kindness.

THE HOUSE OF BLAZE

Paper
is heavy.
With the weight
of thousands of names
on a poetry-petition,
and hundreds of letters
answered with pledges of support,
I hike up a steep hill, climb over
a locked gate, knock on a fancy door
and wait, wait, wait, until suddenly
when it opens, a glaring woman
in a housekeeper's uniform
sweeps me off the porch
with her broom.

I land on a freshly mowed lawn
where a sun-hued cat yawns,
stretches, purrs, and invites me
to cuddle.

OUT LOUD

By the time I stand up
to start walking home,
the power of paper
and a listening ear
strikes me
as a reminder
that just because
I did not achieve my goal YET,
that doesn't mean I won't EVER
succeed.

The orange cat paid close attention
to every moment of my poem-plea reading,
so it was excellent practice
for whatever
   whoever
comes next.

NEXT

My parents advise me to try
the university for statements
by influential experts, but Cat says no,
I should go to a gossipy radio station,
and Gabriela Mistral suggests
that we must walk together
in unity
to the office
of a newspaper
where reporters are writers
who will surely understand
the strength of a poetry-plea
with so many signatures
on powerful paper.

TOGETHER

We must walk together in unity—
those are the words I take special note of
when la poeta makes her suggestion.

If we go as a big crowd,
no one can sweep us away
with a broom.

So we post flyers
announcing our plans
on every bulletin board,
light post, and fence,
that way no one can say
they did not know
we were organizing
a protest.

PROTEST MARCH

We start out slowly
because—as Doris constantly reminds me—
la poeta is diabetic, arthritic, with failing eyesight
and sore knees from kneeling as she scribbles
beneath trees.

At 9:00 a.m. sharp,
people begin to arrive.
Neighbors, strangers.
Cat and Surey don't show up,
neither do
Mima and Papi.
I'm disappointed, but I don't
let that stop me . . .

I stride forward with Alice and Carlitos,
    a leader
of those
who join us along the way,
everyone asking questions
about our purpose.

Kindness
not cruelty,

we repeat over and over
until it becomes a chant
sung to the rhythm
of our footsteps.

WE ROUND A CORNER

. . . and there are my parents,
my sister, her boyfriend,
two excited elephants, one immense,
the other much smaller, yet somehow
both seem almost equally huge,
with a way of moving
that is mountainous
and magical, trunks lifted
as if to catch good luck,
wide feet stomping
narrow tails whisking
floppy ears waving
both massive bodies
swaying, as we all
make our way
through a maze
of honking cars
and amazed
children.

SINGING WITH ELEPHANTS

I hum along
as Chandra and Song
trumpet and rumble
leading our chorus
of animal and human
voices, all of us
inhaling
exhaling
hope
hope
hope
hmmmm
hmmmmm
haaaaaaaaaa

WHEN ELEPHANTS DANCE

People watch
  follow
  learn
  sway, swerve
  swoop, veer
  like a waltz
    rumba
    conga
  the rhythm
of stomping feet and clapping hands
as we chant kindness, not cruelty,
Reunite the family,
Be fair!

DELIVERY

As we approach the newspaper office,
I imagine we look like a circus parade,
but I feel like a diplomat
delivering the weight
of a treaty.

Blaze lives in the land
of rich, famous movie stars
who can do whatever they want,
but Chandra and her twins
come from a realm of animal captives,
fighting for even a tiny fragment
of freedom.

At the very last moment, with reporters
standing right in front of me, I decide
that I'm not the one who should
hand over the poetry-petition
with all those signatures.

You do it, Chandra, I tell the mama elephant.
Surey helps me arrange the tidy stack
into a bundle that she can lift
with the tip of her trunk.

Cameras flash,
reporters scribble
in notebooks,
Gabriela Mistral
nudges me
with her elbow,
and I begin to recite
my poem-plea
OUT
LOUD
to an audience
of listeners.

I know
Abuelita must be proud too,
as she listens, somewhere
far above us.

MY VOICE

"Why is this so important to you?"
"What do you believe Blaze *should* have done?"

Reporters ask me question
after question.
One interview and then another,
I hear myself answering some of them
in English.

My inglés has improved,
my vocabulario has grown.

I still have an accent,
but now I have friends too.

When school starts again,
I'll just spend all my time on the playground
with Carlitos, Alice,
and anyone else
I meet
who is kind
instead of cruel.

FRONT PAGE

My photo
    two elephants
    Blaze . . .

The hero
    the victims
    the villain—
that's how the paper
portrays us.

But really
all I want
is fairness,
he just has to admit
that mimicry is not
language, and tricks
don't justify
loneliness,
and families
should not be
separated.

PERSEVERANCE

The struggle for kindness is not over.
Wishes are made of not only words
but action,
and Dance is still separated
from her mother and brother.

Luckily, it only takes a few more days
to work out solutions
to the elephant family's situation.

The Humane Association agrees to supervise
a reunion of Chandra and her twins, with
a committee of zoologists and veterinarians
filming, to document every detail of behavior
as the isolated baby finally regains
the comfort of natural contact.

Blaze, unfortunately, will be the film's narrator.
A compromise.
Kindness not cruelty, yes,
but still, there are some things I
can't control.

THE POET PACKS HER SUITCASE

I can't control the poet's plans
either.
If only Gabriela Mistral
could stay here forever . . .
but she reminds me that she
will always have to move
from one country to another
like a migrating songbird.

Your voice, she assures me,
has grown both on and off paper,
someday you will be able to speak
and write in ways that you cannot
imagine yet.

I let her words
fill my heart
as tears fill my eyes,
and say goodbye.

MY FUTURE IS BLURRY

but cool shade, the air
where I kneel
beneath trees
is clear.

Gabriela Mistral is right—
I cannot predict the future,
but I can imagine a time
when wild animals
are no longer held captive.

My words and actions
have shown me what
is possible.

Maybe they will change
the whole world
someday.

REUNITED

Days later,
everything is ready—
   cameras
   elephants
   spectators
in place.

The elephant family reunion
is so exhilarating,
shooting stars of happiness
streak all around me
dazzling and sparking
as mother and twins
inhale one another's scent,
wrap their trunks together
swaying, listening
to a melody
only they
can hear.

AUDIENCE

We stand by,
watch the reunion quietly
while experts film, and the liar
narrates, pretending that he
planned this happy moment
all along.

CELEBRATION

Afterward, we invite everyone—
except the liar—to a fiesta of guitars,
Cuban food, and Gabriela Mistral's
poetry, followed by a verse or two
of mine.

My parents can't believe
I've learned so much, and so independently.
Gabriela Mistral gives me a wink.

NEW BEGINNINGS

I leave the festivities early
to walk, walk, walk
las bestiecitas,
tangled leashes
in my hands.

In my heart,
I carry the weight of wishes
that can turn into reality
as I learn how to sing
and dance
on paper.

AUTHOR'S NOTE

All the characters in *Singing with Elephants* are fictional, with the exception of Gabriela Mistral, who was the first Latin American winner of a Nobel Prize for Literature. She lived in Santa Barbara, California, from 1946–1948. I wanted to imagine how she might have influenced a child in that quiet Southern California beach town, so I invented a Cuban immigrant girl who loves animals and nature as much as Mistral.

Gabriela Mistral was born in 1889, in the village of Vicuña, in Chile's mountainous Elqui Valley. She described her ancestry as Inca and Basque. Her name was Lucila de María de Perpetuo Socorro Godoy Alcayaga, but when she began to publish poetry, she chose the pen name Gabriela Mistral. Abused and rejected by old-fashioned teachers, she had no formal education after the age of eleven, so she taught herself, then started working as a teacher when she was fourteen. She believed children deserved kindness, and her reforms of rural education became a model for all of Latin America. At the same time, she became a world-famous poet, and served as a diplomat, representing the government of Chile while living in various countries. In addition, she lectured and taught Spanish literature at universities in the United States, Puerto Rico, Central America, and Uruguay. Well into the twenty-first century, she is still the only Latin American woman winner of the Nobel Prize for Literature.

Along with her literary, educational, and diplomatic careers, Mistral was an influential peace activist. She was one of the founders of the League of Nations and later UNICEF, a branch of the United Nations dedicated to helping women and children. She was an outspoken opponent of xeno-phobia, the fear that leads to violence against foreigners. Even though the police in Brazil ruled her son's death a suicide, she remained convinced that he was murdered by bullies who hated outsiders.

Wherever she went, Mistral befriended children and ani-mals. In Mexico, she was invited to reform the educational system. During later visits, thousands of children sang her poems in one of the world's largest public celebrations of verse.

After leaving Santa Barbara, Mistral traveled to Mexico, Italy, Cuba, and Long Island, New York, where she died in 1957. Her poetry has been translated by famous authors such as Langston Hughes and Ursula K. Le Guin, as well as her companion and secretary, Doris Dana.

In her will, Mistral left the royalties from her books to the children of the Elqui Valley where she was born.

Today, the most unusual tribute to Mistral is an astro-nomic honor rather than a literary one. The Gabriela Mistral Nebula is the only deep space object named after a person it resembles. The Gabriela Mistral Nebula (NGC 3324, found northwest of the Eta Carinae Nebula) is described as a cloud of hydrogen that contains clusters of enormous glowing blue suns. In photographs taken through a powerful telescope, it looks like a profile of Gabriela Mistral's strong, hopeful face.

Even though Oriol, the girl in this story, is imaginary, many of the details of her life are based on reality. For instance, her tiny statue of a wishing elephant comes from a Cuban tradition. I am just one of countless Cubans and Cuban Americans who keep elephant statuettes near windows, with uplifted trunks to catch good luck as it passes, carried by the breeze.

Oriol's native town of whistling bird-walkers was inspired by caged-bird singing competitions and whistled conversations in Silba, a language from the Canary Islands. These traditions survive in various communities on the island of Cuba, including Gibara, on the northeast coast, and my mother's hometown of Trinidad, on the south central coast.

When I was a child growing up in Southern California during the 1950s, we used to visit a wildlife ranch not too far from Santa Barbara. The animals were trained to perform tricks and play roles in Hollywood movies. A few years later, it was closed after accusations of animal abuse. At that time, it was common to see mountain lions for sale in pet stores, chimpanzees languishing in tiny cages at zoos, and elephants forced to contort themselves into unnatural positions at the circus. Even today, macaws and other social birds are taught to mimic human speech by isolating them until they're so lonely that they comply.

Twin elephants are extremely rare. On a few occasions, unscrupulous trainers have attempted to isolate a baby and teach it to mimic human words by moving its tongue with its trunk. Any success with this practice came from the cruelty of imposed loneliness and should never be repeated.

The mother elephant in this book was inspired by a real Asian elephant named Carol, who was friendly and calm, yet inherently wild, and as gentle as the mountain's shadow in Gabriela Mistral's fable *The Elephant and His Secret/El elefante y su secreto*. I had a chance to become friends with Carol while I was working for an irrigation water conservation project at a wildlife breeding facility in California. She amazed me with her ability to use tools, paint pictures, play soccer, and communicate through natural rumbles and hums. However, I was dismayed when I noticed that her mahout (trainer) always carried a heavy metal hook. Modern zoos no longer allow training with tools that cause pain.

All over the world, many nations have banned the use of animals for circus entertainment, and various organizations monitor the filmmaking process to ensure that animals are not harmed during the making of movies.

GABRIELA MISTRAL'S
POETRY FOR CHILDREN

The following is an example of one of Gabriela Mistral's rondas, a rhythmic poem that inspires singing and dancing. This translation is by the famous science fiction author Ursula K. Le Guin:

ANIMALES

Las bestiecitas te rodean
y te balan olfateándote.
De otra tierra y otro reino
llegarían los animales
que parecen niños perdidos,
niños oscuros que cruzasen.
En sus copos de lana y crines,
o en sus careyes relumbrantes,
los cobrizos y los jaspeados
bajan el mundo a pinturearte.
¡Niño del Arca, jueguen contigo,
y hagan su ronda los Animales!

ANIMALS

Small beasts prowl and bleat,
sniffing at your hands and feet.
Another realm, another earth
gave the animals their birth.
Like children seeking home they seem,
dark and passing in a dream.

In their cloudcurled manes and wools,
in their polished shining shells,
coppery or pied or flecked,
they make the world a picturebook.
Child of the Ark, may you hear their call
and dance in the round of the Animals!

FURTHER READING

For children:

Brown, Monica. *My Name Is Gabriela: The Life of Gabriela Mistral/Me llamo Gabriela: la vida de Gabriela Mistral.* Illustrated by John Parra. Monterey, CA: National Geographic School Publishing, 2010.

Mistral, Gabriela. *Crickets and Frogs/Grillos y ranas.* Translated and adapted by Doris Dana. Illustrated by Antonio Frasconi. New York: Atheneum, 1972.

Mistral, Gabriela. *The Elephant and His Secret/El elefante y su secreto.* Translated and adapted by Doris Dana. Illustrated by Antonio Frasconi. New York: Atheneum, 1974.

For adults:

Agosín, Marjorie, editor. *Gabriela Mistral, the Audacious Traveler.* Athens, OH: Ohio University Press, 2003.

Arce de Vazquez, Margot. *Gabriela Mistral: The Poet and Her Work.* New York: New York University Press, 1964.

Mistral, Gabriela. *A Gabriela Mistral Reader.* Translated by Maria Giachetti. Edited by Marjorie Agosín. Fredonia, NY: White Pine Press, 1993.

Mistral, Gabriela. *Madwomen: The "Locas mujeres" Poems of Gabriela Mistral.* Edited and translated by Randall Couch. Chicago: University of Chicago Press, 2008.

Mistral, Gabriela. *Selected Poems of Gabriela Mistral.* Edited and translated by Doris Dana. Illustrated by Antonio Frasconi. Baltimore: Johns Hopkins University Press, 1961.

Mistral, Gabriela. *Selected Poems of Gabriela Mistral.* Edited and translated by Langston Hughes. Bloomington, IN: Indiana University Press, 1957.

Mistral, Gabriela. *Selected Poems of Gabriela Mistral.*

Translated by Ursula K. Le Guin. Albuquerque:
University of New Mexico Press, 2003.

Mistral, Gabriela, and Victoria Ocampo. *This America of
Ours: The Letters of Gabriela Mistral and Victoria Ocampo*.
Edited and translated by Elizabeth Horan and Doris
Meyer. Austin: University of Texas Press, 2003.

Teitelboim, Volodia. *Gabriela Mistral pública y secreta*.
Santiago de Chile: Editorial Sudamericana, 1991.

ACKNOWLEDGMENTS

I thank God for animals, children, poetry, and teachers.

For information about Gabriela Mistral and her house in Santa Barbara, I'm indebted to the Gabriela Mistral Foundation, Santa Barbara Public Library, Joe Cantrell, Consuelo Martínez, and the Hispanic reference section of the Library of Congress. For information about natural elephant communication, I am grateful to *Beyond Words* by Carol Safina (Picador: New York, 2015). For translations of Nepali names, I thank my son-in-law Amish Karanjit. I am profoundly grateful to my husband, Curtis Engle; the rest of my family; my wonderful agent, Michelle Humphrey; my brilliant editor, Liza Kaplan; and the entire publishing team.